THOMAS
AND THE MAGIC RAILROAD ™

based on the feature film *Thomas and the Magic Railroad*

by Britt Allcroft

illustrated by
Tommy Stubbs

Random House 🏠 New York

THOMAS AND THE MAGIC RAILROAD created by Britt Allcroft. By Britt Allcroft.
Including THOMAS THE TANK ENGINE & FRIENDS. Based on The Railway Series by The Rev W Awdry.
All underlying rights worldwide Britt Allcroft (Thomas) LLC. Copyright © The Magic Railroad Company Limited 2000.
THOMAS AND THE MAGIC RAILROAD is a trademark of Britt Allcroft Inc in the USA, Mexico, and Canada and of
The Magic Railroad Company Limited in the rest of the world. THE BRITT ALLCROFT COMPANY is a trademark of
The Britt Allcroft Company plc. All rights reserved under International and Pan-American Copyright Conventions.
Published in the United States of America by Random House, Inc., New York, and simultaneously in Canada
by Random House of Canada Limited, Toronto.
RANDOM HOUSE and colophon are registered trademarks of Random House, Inc.

www.randomhouse.com/kids   www.thomasthetankengine.com

Library of Congress Cataloging-in-Publication Data
Allcroft, Britt.   Thomas and the magic railroad / by Britt Allcroft.
p.   cm. — "Based on the feature film Thomas and the magic railroad."
SUMMARY: Thomas the Tank Engine makes a perilous trip to bring back Lady, the Golden Engine, and restore the Magic Railroad to life.
ISBN 0-375-80551-6
[1. Railroads—Trains—Fiction. 2. Magic—Fiction.]
I. Title. PZ7.A4143Th 2000 [E]—dc21 99-085990
Printed in the United States of America June 2000 10 9 8 7 6 5 4 3 2 1

Thomas the Tank Engine is a little blue engine who lives on the Island of Sodor. He has many engine friends, and they all try to be Really Useful.

There was harmony on the Island of Sodor until, one day, a mean diesel engine arrived. He was called Diesel 10, and he hated steam engines.

"Get out of my way, you puffballs!" he growled as he sped past Thomas and Gordon the Express Engine. "When I'm done with my plan, you'll be nothing but useless scrap!"

Thomas was scared of Diesel 10, but he knew he had to be a brave little engine.

Far away from the Island of Sodor, across a wide ocean and on the other side of Muffle Mountain, was the town of Shining Time. It was the home of Mr. Conductor, who comes and goes in gold dust.

Mr. Conductor was getting ready for a trip to the Island of Sodor on the Magic Railroad. The Magic Railroad was a Conductor Family Secret.

The engines were very glad to see their friend Mr. Conductor. He would take care of them while Sir Topham Hatt, the railroad director, went on vacation.

But Diesel 10 had other plans.

"I'll soon settle Twinkle-Toes with my claw," he snarled.

That night, Diesel 10 sidled up to the shed while Mr. Conductor and the engines were asleep.

"Gold dust...magic...buffers," Mr. Conductor mumbled in his dreams. He woke up remembering what his family had always told him: *As long as there is gold dust, there will be harmony.* He blew his whistle, but it had no sparkle.

"Oh, no," cried Mr. Conductor. "I've got to find more gold dust to run the railroad or we will all be in danger!"

Diesel 10 slunk quietly away.

Using a bellflower, Mr. Conductor called his cousin Junior and told him to fetch the emergency supply of gold dust from Shining Time Station.

About that time, a young girl named Lily arrived at Shining Time, led by a friendly dog called Mutt. Lily had come from the Big City to visit her grandpa, Burnett Stone, who lived on Muffle Mountain.

The trains didn't stop on Burnett's side of the mountain, but that night Lily heard the sound of a train whistle outside her window.

The next morning, Thomas went to fetch coal for Henry, who had boiler ache. The last freight car wasn't coupled properly to the others. It glided through an old set of buffers and disappeared.

Meanwhile, a very tired Mr. Conductor was searching for the source of the gold dust. Diesel 10 caught him walking along a viaduct. Diesel 10 grabbed Mr. Conductor with his claw and dangled him over the gorge! Mr. Conductor yanked out his pliers and cut one of the cables connected to Diesel 10's claw.

The claw sprang open and flung Mr. Conductor onto a sack of grain at the base of a windmill. There he found a clue to the source of the gold dust. It said: *Stoke up the magic in the mountain, and the Lady will smile. Then watch the swirls that spin so well.*

Back at Shining Time Station, Lily met Mr. Conductor's cousin Junior. He appeared in a wonderful cascade of sparkles. Junior was on his way to the Island of Sodor. He asked Lily to go with him.

"I'll use the last of my cousin's gold dust," said Junior. "It's the only way to travel, and we'll find lots more soon."

Whoosh! Suddenly, they were on the Magic Railroad, moving bumpily along. The gold dust made little pools of light in the dark tunnel.

The two of them glided right through the buffers at the end of the track. Lily's eyes widened when she saw the Island of Sodor in all its marvelous magic.

"I was at the old buffers when the last coal car disappeared," Thomas was saying to Percy.

"Then I think those buffers are the entrance to Mr. Conductor's Magic Railroad!" Percy said excitedly.

"Percy, you are clever!" said Thomas. "Now keep the buffers safe while I search for Mr. Conductor."

To Thomas' surprise, he found Junior instead! Junior introduced Thomas to the astonished Lily. She couldn't believe that trains could talk! In no time at all, Thomas was puffing along with Lily and Junior on board. Junior spotted his cousin at the bottom of the windmill.

"Howdy, cuz," Junior said.

Mr. Conductor smiled and gave his cousin a hug.

In his darkened workshop, Burnett Stone was working on the beautiful golden steam engine called Lady. It was Lady's whistle that Lily had heard that night.

When Burnett was young, Lady was hurt in a terrible accident. Lady's beautiful face had faded, and the Magic Railroad faded with it. As hard as he tried, Burnett couldn't make Lady come back to life.

"The railroad needs Lady," whispered Burnett as he worked. "I need to know the secret to make her run again."

On the Island of Sodor, Diesel 10 was plotting to destroy the Magic Railroad.

"We don't know which buffers are the entrance to the Magic Railroad," he told his hench-diesels, Splatter and Dodge. "We'll just have to destroy them all!"

Percy overheard the diesels' plan and knew the engines had to act quickly.

"We must get Lily back to Muffle Mountain before the diesels destroy the Magic Railroad," Percy said.

"Without gold dust, the only way to travel the Magic Railroad is on the lost engine, Lady," said Mr. Conductor. "Unless…Thomas, you're a Really Useful Engine. You can do it."

"I'll try," Thomas said bravely.

As Thomas and Lily chugged toward the magic buffers, Mr. Conductor called after them, *Stoke up the magic in the mountain, and the Lady will smile."*

They reached the buffers—and went right through them, onto the Magic Railroad! They spotted the missing coal car and quickly coupled it to Thomas.

Looming up ahead was a huge set of buffers. Thomas and Lily passed right through them onto Muffle Mountain! Lily jumped off Thomas and ran to Burnett's workshop.

Elsewhere on Muffle Mountain, a huge explosion jolted Thomas off the ground and onto another branch of the Magic Railroad. In this unfamiliar place, Thomas wasn't sure he could find his way back to where he'd left Lily. He hurried off to find a connection back to the main line.

At the same time, Lily rushed into Burnett's workshop, where she saw the beautiful golden engine. "This is the lost engine from long ago!" exclaimed Lily. "She's the key to Mr. Conductor's Magic Railroad."

"I don't know how to make Lady run," said Burnett sadly. But Lily suddenly realized that *she* did.

"She needs coal from the Island of Sodor!" Lily said. "Thomas and I brought some with us."

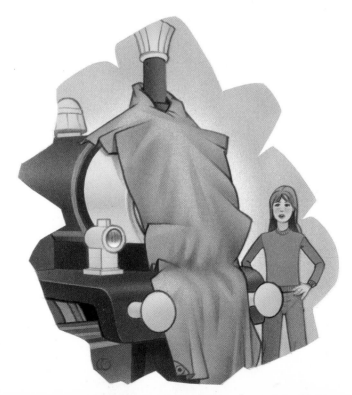

Soon, Lady was steaming along the Magic Railroad. As she gathered speed, her lovely face was revealed once again.

"Stoke up the magic in the mountain, and the Lady will smile," Lily murmured to herself.

The railroad's energy was returning. Shavings all the colors of the rainbow fell behind Lady and gathered on the ground.

Lily caught some shavings in her backpack. Then she saw Thomas about to meet up with the Magic Railroad's main line. As the shimmering shavings settled on the rusty tracks, Thomas gained traction and gathered speed.

With a long, low roar, Lady burst through the buffers onto the Island of Sodor!

Burnett, Lily, and Mutt jumped off Lady to join the others. Then Thomas burst through the buffers right behind Lady.

Suddenly, Diesel 10 appeared, as if from nowhere. With a roar, he rushed at Thomas, his jagged claw snapping.

"I'll get you, puffball," yelled Diesel 10. "And I'll get that magic engine, too!"

"Run, Lady, quickly—I'll help you!" called Thomas.

Burnett leaped into Lady's cab, and they sped toward an old viaduct.

Thomas raced between Lady and Diesel 10. As Lady crossed the viaduct, it began to crumble, and a hole opened in the track ahead of Thomas. Thomas bravely jumped the gap! But as Diesel 10 closed in, the rest of the viaduct collapsed.

"*Noooooooo!*" screamed Diesel 10.

Diesel 10 slid over the edge of the viaduct and dropped onto a barge filled with sludge. Off he floated, never to be seen again.

Lily opened her backpack and scooped out the wonderful shavings from the railroad. *"Stoke up the magic in the mountain, and the Lady will smile..."*

"Then watch the swirls that spin so well," Mr. Conductor recited, remembering the rest of the clue to the gold dust.

"So well! A well means water!" shouted Junior.

Lily mixed the shavings with Sodor water and shook them around, as if panning for gold. Then she threw the mixture into the air.

"Gold dust!" everyone yelled.

Back at the magic buffers, Mr. Conductor and Junior recovered their sparkle with the new gold dust. Lily and her grandfather hugged each other with joy.

It was a happy Thomas who puffed home that evening, knowing that a little blue engine like himself had been so very *useful.*